Happy Halloween!

To:
From:

Dedicated to my parents and grandparents

Jack and the O'Lanterns by Victoria Yurachek
Published by Victoria Yurachek
Copyright © 2020 Victoria Yurachek
All rights reserved

For information regarding permission, write to booksbyvictoriay@gmail.com.
Paperback: 978-1-7341612-0-5, E-book: 978-1-7341612-1-2
Library of Congress Control Number: 2020931860
Cover art and illustration by Leysan Shayakbirova

Jack and his band practice all year long.
The O'Lanterns play as Jack sings a song.

They practice for the Halloween Talent Show.
Spooks will perform for every haunt they know.

The day arrives. The talent show is here.
As they peek from backstage, their turn gets near.

Vampire recites funny jokes.

The witches perform a magic trick.

The O'Lanterns come after Werewolf,
jumping on his pogo stick.

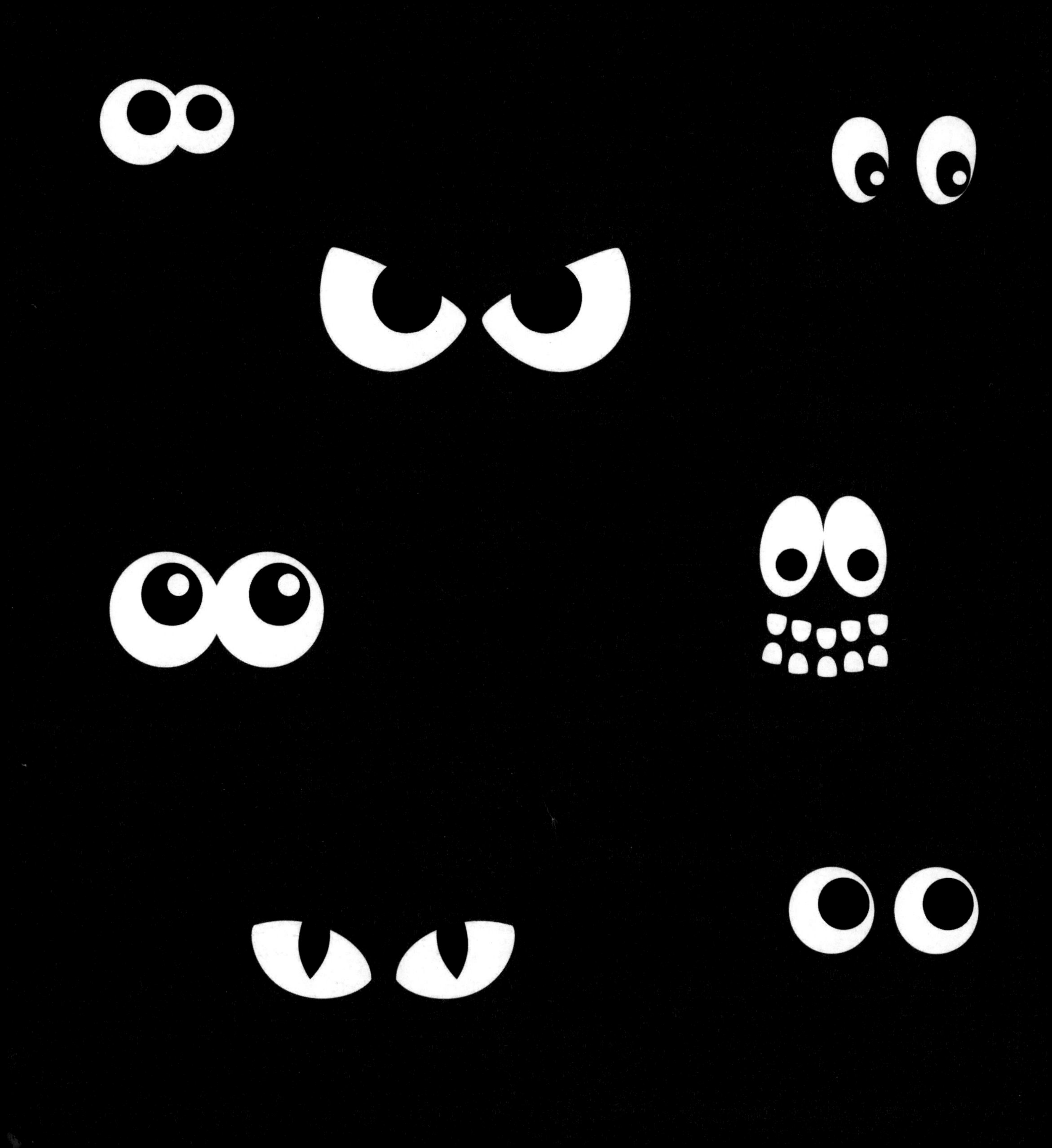

An unexpected storm arrives! The hall is dark as it can be.
Suddenly all the lights go out. Now no one in the crowd can see!

Will the show end early? What should they do?
The O'Lanterns worked hard. They must pull through.

Jack turns to his band. He knows just what to say.
He mentions his idea so the talent show can stay.

"We can still perform! We'll light up the hall!
We aren't just pumpkins, after all!"

Their faces light up. Everyone is in shock.
They can still play music and all can rock!

The crowd yells and cheers since the music is grand.
Jack and the O'Lanterns are heroes and more than just a band!

Victoria Yurachek

is from Illinois. Her favorite holiday is Halloween. She loves carving pumpkins and creating fun, unique costumes. The cat in *Jack and the O'Lanterns* is inspired by her cat, Blackie. Victoria is also the author of ***The Beagles' Bagel Shop***.

Leysan Shayakbirova

is an illustrator from Kazan, Russia. She lives with her cat and horse. She enjoys creating cute and funny illustrations for children. Leysan has illustrated numbers of educational and picture books for children.

Made in the USA
Monee, IL
06 March 2020